Investigator™

in

New Ghouls on the Block

by Jerry Smath

Troll Associates

Dear Reader,
    You can be an investigator, too! Just figure
out the puzzles that appear throughout the
story, and help Investigator solve the mystery
of *New Ghouls on the Block.*

To Louis Bacigalupo
—J.S.

Investigator was busy decorating the house for a Halloween party when the doorbell rang.

It was Investigator's nephew Newton and his niece Gabby. They were with their friends, but Newton and Gabby were not dressed for Halloween.

"Can you make us costumes so we can go out trick-or-treating?" asked Gabby.

★ Can you find ten pumpkins?
★ How many are happy?
★ How many are angry?

"Of course I can!" said Investigator.
Quicker than you can say **BOO,** Investigator made each of them a wonderful costume.

"Can we go trick-or-treating before the party?" asked Newton.

"Okay," said Investigator, "but wait until I finish decorating the house and I will go with you."

But the kids did not wait. When Investigator wasn't looking they went out trick-or-treating by themselves.

★ Which kid has the most treats?
★ Which kid's bag has a hole in it?

When Investigator finished his work, his little friends were nowhere to be found.

Investigator went outside to look for them. There he saw Gabby and her friends running toward him.

"Newton is gone!" cried Gabby. "He went into a spooky old house down the street and he never came out!"

Investigator sprang into action. "Come with me in the van and show me the house!"

★ How many owls can you find?
★ How many owls are sleeping?
★ Whose bag has fallen?

Investigator turned on his siren and drove down the ghoulishly decorated streets.

"We're almost there!" shouted Gabby. "It's just around the next corner."

★ Can you find something wrong with each house?

In a few minutes, Investigator and his friends arrived at the old house.

"Stay in the van!" said the world's greatest detective as he headed down the walkway. "I will soon get to the bottom of this!"

★ How many stones are missing from the walkway?
★ Match each missing stone to its hole.
★ Can you find six broken things on the house?

Investigator found Newton's hat lying on the front porch. He knocked on the big front door. It swung open with a loud creak.

"Newton!" he called. No one answered.

"I feel as if I'm being watched," said Investigator.

★ Investigator is right! There are 11 things watching him. Can you find them?

Investigator heard noises coming from a big box
in the corner of the room.

"Is that you, Newton?" he called.

Investigator took out his special box-lid lifter and
pushed down on the handle.

POP went the lid of the box. Out came all kinds
of creepy things.

But no Newton.

★ How many blue bats can you find?
★ Find six spotted ghosts.
★ Find seven sneaky snakes.

"*Hee-hee-hee!*"

Investigator heard spooky laughter coming from upstairs. He dashed up the stairs, rushing past all sorts of strange pictures on the wall.

"Yipes!" cried Investigator when he reached the landing. "A ghost!"

★ There is a picture missing from the wall. Do you know where it once hung?
★ Do the two monsters in the picture look exactly alike?
★ Can you find six skulls?
★ Where do each of the colored glass panes go?

At the top of the stairs Investigator saw a door. He pushed it open.

Inside the room was a really scary sight. Monsters, ghosts, and ghouls of all sizes stood waving their arms, wings, and legs at Investigator. They made terrible growling noises. Nearby, a suspicious-looking duck tinkered with a robot.

DR. QUACKER'S WORK SHOP

★ Which head on the shelf belongs to the robot?
★ The strange creatures are all plugged in.
  Which wire goes to which creature?

Investigator knew just what to do. He reached into his bag and pulled out a mirror.

"You can't scare me!" said Investigator, "but I can scare you!"

Investigator held up his mirror. All the creatures could see their own reflections.

"YEEEOW!" the creatures screamed. They all ran away.

"Stop!" the duck screamed. "You're ruining my wonderful inventions!"

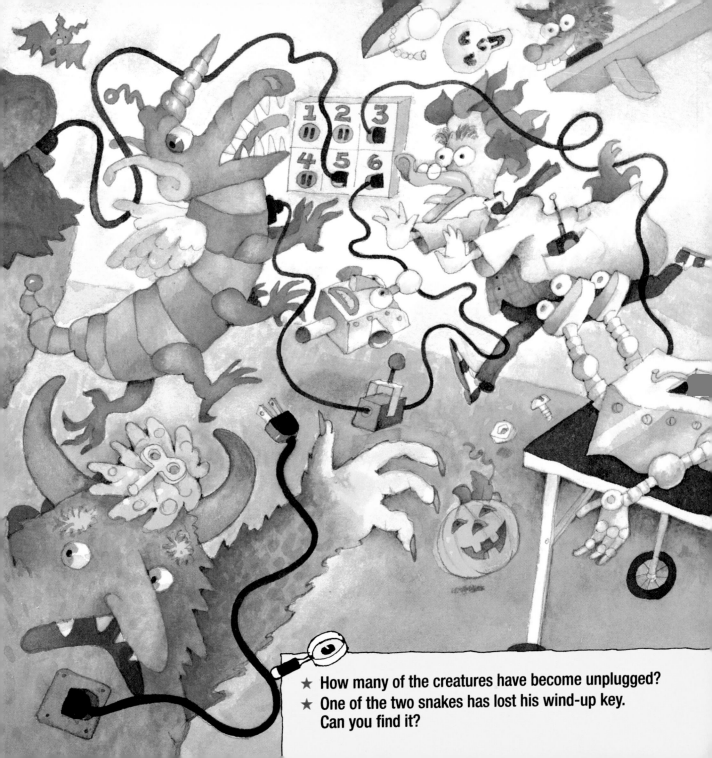

★ How many of the creatures have become unplugged?
★ One of the two snakes has lost his wind-up key. Can you find it?

Investigator took Newton's hat from his bag and waved it at the duck.

"Who are you?" he shouted. "And where is my nephew?"

"I am Dr. Quacker, the inventor," said the duck. "Your nephew is no longer here."

"Then where is he?" demanded Investigator.

★ Can you find four bats that are hiding?
★ What looks different about Investigator's hat?

Dr. Quacker smiled and took a black box from his pocket.

"Would you like to join your nephew?" he asked.

Dr. Quacker pushed a red button on the box. Investigator suddenly disappeared down a hole in the floor.

★ Dr. Quacker has lost something. What is it?
★ Can you find the missing object?

Investigator slid down a long tunnel and landed outside on a soft pillow in the yard.

When he looked up, Newton was standing over him.

"Hi, Uncle!" said Newton, who was holding three balloons and a bucket filled with candy. "Isn't Dr. Quacker the greatest? Look at all the Halloween treats he gave me!"

★ There are ten lollipops in this picture. Can you find them?
★ How many birds are hiding?

Gabby and her friends were happy to see Newton again.

"I guess Dr. Quacker isn't so strange after all," Investigator said.

"But his house sure is!" added Newton.

Everyone laughed as Investigator drove home.

"Wait! Stop!" Newton suddenly shouted. "I left my treats in Dr. Quacker's yard."

Investigator turned the van around and headed back to the spooky old house.

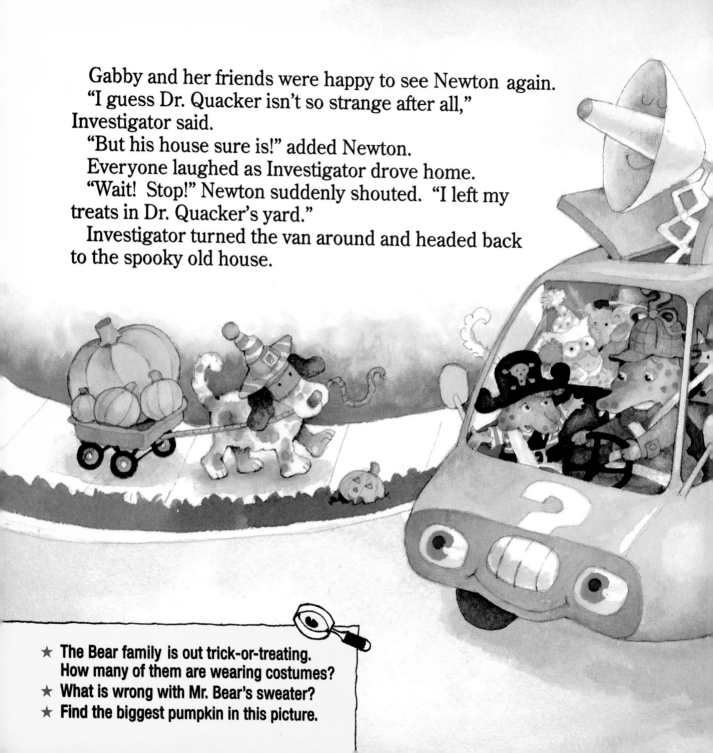

★ **The Bear family is out trick-or-treating. How many of them are wearing costumes?**
★ **What is wrong with Mr. Bear's sweater?**
★ **Find the biggest pumpkin in this picture.**

But then a strange thing happened.

When Investigator drove up to Dr. Quacker's house — it wasn't there!

Investigator saw some tracks on the grass and road. He carefully examined them.

"Hmmm," he said. "I think I know where Dr. Quacker and his house have gone!"

★ What kind of tracks do you think Investigator found?

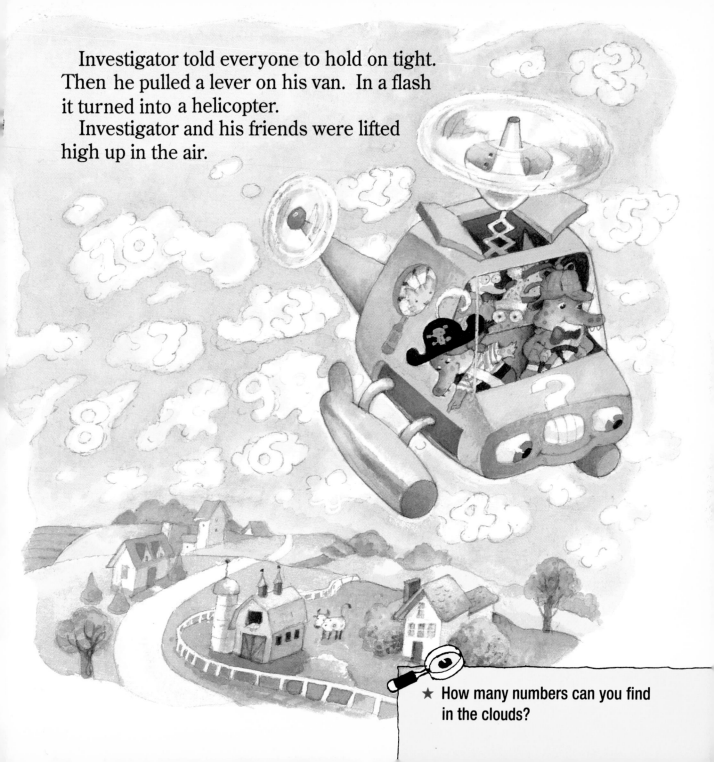

Investigator told everyone to hold on tight. Then he pulled a lever on his van. In a flash it turned into a helicopter.

Investigator and his friends were lifted high up in the air.

★ How many numbers can you find in the clouds?

"Look down!" said Investigator. "There is Dr. Quacker and his mysterious house!"

"He looks like he's on his way to join the carnival!" yelled Gabby and Newton.

"You two are so smart," said their uncle with a smile.

CARNIVAL

GAS

GAS

★ Which sign is wrong?
★ How many cars are going to the carnival?
How many cars are coming back?
★ Which cars have broken down?

Back home Investigator helped the children eat their Halloween treats.

"You've done it again, Uncle," said Newton. "You've solved the mystery of the new ghouls on the block."

Everyone laughed.

"It only goes to prove," said Newton, "that there's no detective greater than Investigator!"

★ Where is one kid hiding?
★ Bunny has lost the star from her magic wand. Can you find it?
★ Who ate too many treats?